T0370481

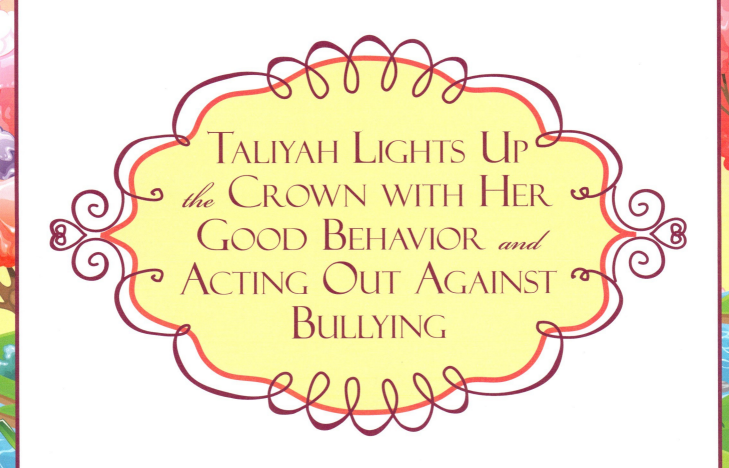

Taliyah Lights Up the Crown with Her Good Behavior and Acting Out Against Bullying

Phyllis L. Morris-Holmes

Illustrators April Johnson and Taliyah Holmes.

AuthorHouse™
1663 Liberty Drive
Bloomington, IN 47403
www.authorhouse.com
Phone: 1 (800) 839-8640

Published by AuthorHouse 06/13/2016

ISBN: 978-1-5049-8340-2 (sc)
978-1-5049-8341-9 (e)

Library of Congress Control Number: 2016903674

Print information available on the last page.

Any people depicted in stock imagery provided by Thinkstock are models,
and such images are being used for illustrative purposes only.
Certain stock imagery © Thinkstock.

This book is printed on acid-free paper.

authorHOUSE®

Taliyah Lights the Crown Acting Out Against Bullying

By the Spirit of the Lord that moves within me,

That provides my every need,

And has blessed me with this idea,

I dedicate this book to my

Granddaughter, Taliyah.

A Good Girl Named Taliyah
Powers the Crown that Lights Up!

By Phyllis Morris-Holmes

©2011

All Rights Reserved

The forest of **Look and See** looked very scary, but Grandma was on a mission to get her Princess Granddaughter Taliyah a very special crown.

When Princess Taliyah is good and very good her special crown will light up!

When Taliyah is a good little girl WHO acts like a Princess, with very good behavior, (especially in school), her crown will light up for all the world to see.

Grandma teamed up with two wonderful friends to go on an adventure in the forest of **Look and See**.

Grandma's first friend was a frog named Good.

He took Grandma by the hand and told her, "if you are also, good, all the animals in the forest will help you find the Crown that Lights Up."

Grandma was on her best behavior so they were having a great adventure.

So Grandma and Good the Frog went hand in hand deeper into the Forest.

Grandma was not afraid to go into the forest because she was with her friend, Good the Frog.

Grandma and Good the Frog were singing and laughing as they walked further into the forest.

All of a sudden there was a loud sound that came from behind a big oak tree.

A voice said real loudly, "What are you two doing in my forest?" Grandma stood real still and stayed quiet right behind her friend, Good the Frog, because she was so afraid of the loud sound and unknown voice.

Good the Frog took her hand and told her not to be afraid. He would go and see what that loud sound was and the unknown voice.

So Good the Frog leaped over the tree and said, "Who is behind this tree?"
"It is I", said the voice. "And who are you"? asked Good the Frog.

"It is I, Acting Out," a scrappy little voice said. "Why are you so loud?" asked Good, the Frog. "You scared my friend, Grandma."

"I'm always loud" said Acting Out, "because I want to be noticed by everyone." "Well, come from behind the tree so we can see you."

So Acting Out came from behind the tree and Grandma and Good the Frog were surprised to see a little wiggly worm.

Grandma and Good the Frog said to Acting Out, the little wiggly worm, "Well you can be noticed without being loud. We are noticing you right now talking loud."

"Well, that is so true," said Acting Out, the little wiggly worm. "Maybe I don't have to be loud to be noticed. I can just be myself." "Yes," said Grandma and Good the Frog. "Just be yourself and you will still get noticed."

"Would you like to go on an adventure with Grandma and me?" asked Good the Frog.

"We are going to go deep into the forest of **Look and See** to find a special crown for Grandma's Granddaughter, Taliyah."

"What is so special about this crown?" asked Acting Out the little wiggly worm.

"Well, when Taliyah is wearing the crown and has good behavior, the most amazing thing happens," said Grandma.

"What! What happens?" asked Acting Out the little wiggly worm.

"Well the Crown Lights Up."

"Oh yes please," said Acting Out the little wiggly worm. "I would love to go on an adventure with you into the forest of **Look and See**."

"Well," said Grandma and Good the Frog, "there are some rules you will have to follow. Are you willing to follow them they asked Acting Out?"

"Oh Yes, Oh Yes," said Acting Out. "Okay there are three rules that you must follow" said Good the Frog.

"The first rule is you cannot be loud because you will scare the other animals in the forest."

"Oh, I can do that;" said Acting Out the little wiggly worm. "I will be so quiet that I will not make a sound."

"Great!" said Grandma. "Now tell Acting Out the second rule that he must follow.

"The second rule is you must always listen to Grandma and me when we tell you to do something," said Good the frog. "You must be on your best behavior."

"Well, I can do that to," said Acting Out the little wiggly worm. See how good I am being now?"

"Well, yes you are," said Grandma.

"So I know that you will be a great listener too, and will put on your listening ears."

"Now here's the last and final rule," said Good the Frog.

No matter what you see or hear, do not run when you are not suppose to because you can hurt yourself and us too. Remember you must always listen to instructions."

"Well, I promise not to run when I am suppose to walk. I do not want to hurt myself, and I really do not want to hurt you, Good the Frog, or Grandma. I will be on my best behavior and follow all the rules, all the time," said Acting Out the little wiggly worm.

"Remember, we want to find the Crown that Lights Up for Grandma's Granddaughter, Taliyah. We want everyone to see how great she is because her Good behavior is the power that lights up the crown."

Acting Out, the little wiggly worm, agreed to practice good behavior, to listen all the time, and not to run when he is not supposed to. He again promised to follow all the rules. He was so excited to be going on an adventure into the forest of **Look and See**.

So off they went, Grandma, Good the Frog, and Acting Out, the little wiggly worm.

They Walked, and walked, and walked deep into the forest of **Look and See**.

Deep within the forest, they all stopped to **Look and See** the wonderful animals in the Forest. All the animals were nice to them and they were nice to the animals.

Even Acting Out, the little wiggly worm, was following all the rules that Grandma and Good the Frog gave to him.

As they walked along they came upon a beautiful tree with colors of the rainbow.

They had never seen anything so beautiful. So they stopped to look and see all the beautiful colors. They were so amazed and in awe of its beauty that they were startled when a voice said, "What are you looking at?" "Are you lost in the forest of **Look and See**?"

They all answered at the same time... "We are looking at a rainbow tree. We have never seen anything like it." "Oh!" said the sweet voice of the prettiest kitten you could ever imagine. (And because he was so nice, his name was Nice.)

"We animals in the forest are so used to seeing Rainbow Tree all the time that we forget how beautiful she is to others. But you did not answer my other question. Are you lost?"

"Yes." Said Grandma, Good the Frog, and Acting Out. "We are looking for the Crown that Lights Up. We are going to give it to Grandma's Granddaughter, Taliyah to wear and the power of her good behavior will light up the crown for all the world to see."

"I can help you find it quickly," said Nice, the prettiest little kitten you could imagine, "but we all have to work together to open up the pearl chest that holds the crown inside it. It is very hard to open."

Acting Out, the little wiggly worm shouted, "I want to help too!" and Grandma and Good the Frog said, "Okay, but do not shout. You have been so good with your behavior during our adventure into the forest of **Look and See.**"

"We are very proud of you," said Good the Frog and Grandma. Acting Out was very proud too and was never loud again.

So Grandma, Good the Frog, Acting out, the little wiggly worm and Nice, the prettiest Kitten you can imagine found the pearl chest.

Working together they got the pearl chest open. Because they worked together in a group and helped each other it was so easy to do.

Grandma was so happy when she finally had the Crown. She was so excited and looked forward to giving it to her Granddaughter Taliyah to wear. Grandma knew that when her Granddaughter Taliyah wears the Crown, that her good behavior in school, good behavior at home, good behavior in church, good behavior in her community, and good behavior everywhere she goes is the power that Lights up the Crown for all the world to see.

Then Grandma thanked Good the Frog, Acting Out, the little wiggly worm, and Nice, the prettiest Kitten you can imagine for all their help.

She was so glad that she went into the forest of **Look and See** and found the best gift for her Granddaughter Taliyah, the Crown that Lights Up with Good Behavior!

Questions that Grandma, Good the Frog, Acting Out, the little wiggly worm and Nice the Kitten want to know.

What did your Grandmother get you that was so special?

_____

_____

_____

Why?

_____

_____

_____

What did you think of the little wiggly worm?

_____

_____

_____

What did you like about Good the Frog?

_____

_____

_____

What did you like about Nice, the prettiest little kitten you can imagine?

_____

_____

_____

Have you ever seen a rainbow tree?

_____

_____

_____

Have you ever seen a rainbow?

_____

_____

_____

What are some of the animals that live in a forest?

_____

_____

_____

Have you seen a treasure chest?

_____

_____

_____

What were the three rules that the little wiggly worm had to follow?

_____

_____

_____

How many rules do you follow?

_____

_____

_____

What are they?

_____

_____

_____

What part of the story did you like best?

_____

_____

_____

Why?

_____

_____

_____

Who are some of your best friends?

_____

_____

_____

Why?

_____

_____

_____

Where do you have good behavior?

_____

_____

_____

Acting Out
Against Bullying

Grandma was at home reading her favorite book, **"A Good Girl Named Taliyah Powers the Crown that Lights Up"** when her phone rang. Now who could that be, said Grandma, as she was really enjoying the book.

"Hello," Grandma said. "Whom am I talking with?" "It's me", said Nice, the prettiest little kitten you could even imagine. Well how are you doing since our adventure into the forest of **Look and See**, asked Grandma?

"I am doing great, said Nice, the prettiest little kitten you could ever imagine. I have gone back twice to the forest of **Look and See** to visit Rainbow Tree."

It is still the prettiest tree that I have even seen. "Well I certainly agree with you on that", said Grandma. "So how are you doing" Grandma, asked Nice, the prettiest little Kitten you could imagine?

Well, I am so glad to tell you that my Granddaughter Taliyah's good behavior keeps that crown lit up, said Grandma laughing.

You know her good behavior is the power that lights up the crown. Oh that is so great, said Nice, the prettiest little Kitten you could ever imagine. I am so glad that her good behavior is on display for the whole world to see.

"It's so nice to hear from you", said Grandma. What can I do for you? Well I need you to gather our friends, Good, the Frog, and Acting Out, the little wiggly worm.

We need to go on another adventure back into the forest of **Look and See**.

"Oh good," said Grandma," I love going on adventures. What will our mission be?" asked Grandma.

We are going to help the animals that live in the forest of **Look and See**. What is going on in the forest asked Grandma.

I will tell you once we are all together, said Nice, the prettiest little Kitten you could ever imagine.

When you call Good, the Frog, and Acting Out, the wiggly little worm, tell them we will all meet at the entrance into the forest of **Look and See**. I will tell everyone the mission then said Nice, the prettiest little Kitten you could ever imagine.

So Grandma and Nice, the prettiest kitten you could ever imagine, said their goodbyes, with the promise to see each other soon.

Grandma immediately called Good, the Frog, and Acting Out, the wiggly little worm. She told them to meet her and Nice, the prettiest little kitten you could ever imagine at the entrance of the forest of **Look and See**.

They were going on a new adventure.

So Grandma, Good, the Frog, Acting Out, the wiggly little worm, and Nice, the prettiest little kitten you could ever imagine all met up at the entrance into the forest of **Look and See**.

Upon seeing Nice, Grandma asked, "what is this mission all about?"

We are going to help the animals in the forest of **Look and See** said Nice, the prettiest little kitten you could ever imagine. How can we help the animals asked Grandma and good the Frog?

"Can I help too?" asked Acting Out, the little wiggly worm.

Oh yes, said Nice, we can all help the animals in the forest. There is a small band of bullying animals deep in the forest of **Look and See**.

It seems that all the animals share and drink water from the little river stream; it is so peaceful, calm, and clean. All the animals drink from this stream of love.

Well that sounds like a nice place to get a drink of water. So how can we help said Grandma, Good the Frog, and Acting Out, the wiggly little worm?

Nice, the prettiest little kitten you could imagine, stated that the small band of bullying animals stand around the stream of Love and will only let the animals have a drink of water, if they bring them their favorite food.

"How long has this been going on, asked Grandma? It just started said Nice, the prettiest little kitten you could imagine. That's why we have to put a stop to it right away."

Acting Out, the little wiggly worm wiggled more and more and almost got stuck because he was so mad.

"What right do they have to bully these animals when the stream of Love is for all the animals to drink from," said Acting out, the wiggly little worm.

"Oh dear," said Grandma to Acting Out, "don't get so angry. You'll tie yourself into knots."

We will all work together to help the animals in the forest of **Look and See**.

By the time we get done, every animal in the forest will once again drink from the Stream of Love.

"Okay," said Acting Out. "I will not lose my temper again. I will stay calm so that I can hear what we are going to do."

"Very good," said Grandma and Good the Frog.

Okay Nice, tell us more about the bullying animals. Who is their leader? Nice, the prettiest little kitten you can imagine, said their leader is a stripe, a small, smelly skunk.

He threatens the animals with his smelling power. He will let out the stinkiest smell ever if they try drinking from the Stream of Love.

"Oh my, said Grandma. That is not very nice." Who else is being a bully?

Well, there is So-So, the slithering snake. He is telling the animals that he will wrap himself around their bodies if they try to drink from the Stream of Love.

That's not very nice either, said Good the Frog. We really need to help the animals in the forest of **Look and See**.

Is there anyone else who is being a bully? Asked Grandma.

Yes, said Nice, the prettiest kitten you can imagine. His name is Raspy, the roaring Lion. He roars so loud when one of our animal friends tries to drink from the Stream of Love and his roaring hurts your ears.

"Well now," said Grandma to Good the frog, Acting Out, the little wiggly worm, and Nice, the prettiest little kitten you could ever imagine, "as I said earlier, this is not going to be an easy mission."

But you know, because we work so well together, and we listen to each other, we will all come up with great ideas and a wonderful plan so that the animals in the forest of **Look and See** will be able to enjoy the Stream of Love in peace.

Acting Out, the little wiggly worm said to Grandma, I want to come up with a plan on my own.

Will you Good the Frog, and Nice, the prettiest little kitten you could ever imagine trust me to do it?

Oh yes, said Grandma, Good the Frog, and Nice, the prettiest little kitten you could ever imagine. We will trust you because we know that everyone has a special gift.

So Acting Out, the little wiggly worm, put on his thinking cap. He said that he would think and come up with his plan. He sat very still, closed his eyes. He was waiting to listen to that still small voice that would tell him what to do.

While being very still he asked how he could teach So-So, the slithering snippy snake, Raspy, the roaring lion, and Stripe, the smelly skunk that what they were doing was not very nice.

Acting Out thought, and he thought, and he thought. He thought so long that Grandma, Good the Frog, and Nice, the prettiest little kitten you could imagine thought that he was asleep.

Finally, just when they could take no more, Acting Out opened his eyes and wiggled. "I've got it!" He asked Grandma, Good, the Frog, and Nice, the prettiest little kitten you could ever imagine to gather all the animals in the forest of **Look and See**.

When all the animals were together, Acting Out told them all to go to the Stream of Love together, to drink at the same time, and only bring food for Stripe, the smelly skunk.

The animals went together deep into the forest of **Look and See** to first search for food for Stripe, the smelly skunk. They gathered together berries, roots, and some nuts. On their way to the Stream of Love they laughed and played together.

Upon reaching the Stream of Love, Stripe, the smelly skunk was already there. At first the animals were afraid. Then they remembered what Grandma said, to just be you, to be nice, and to give Stripe, the smelly skunk some food.

When Stripe, the smelly skunk saw all the wonderful berries, roots, and nuts, he let all the animals drink from the Stream of Love. The animals did this for three days.

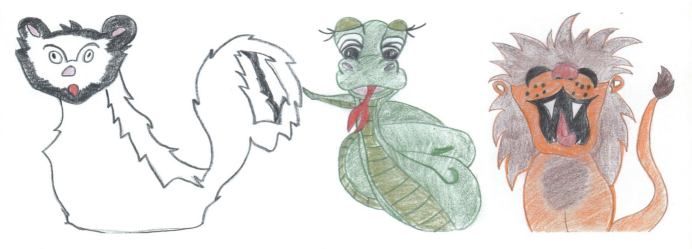

By the third day, So-So, the slithering snake and Raspy, the roaring Lion were very, very hungry.

Acting Out put his other plan in action. He went first to So-So, the slithering snake and said your good friend, Stripe, the smelly skunk has been getting the food he loves for three whole days. Did he tell the other animals to bring you your favorite food?

So-So, the slithering snake thought and thought. He looked over at where Stripe, the smelly skunk, was sleeping in the sun. His friend Stripes belly was full and he even had a smile on his face.

So-So, the slithering snake finally started thinking for himself. He realized that Stripe the smelly skunk was only looking out for himself. He was not really being a good friend because friends don't hurt each other. He also knew that they certainly don't threaten or hurt others just because of their own special powers.

So-So, the slithering snake no longer wanted to be a part of bullying the other animals because it was not worth it. He decided from that point on that he would join everyone else when they went to drink from the Stream of Love. He also wanted to apologize to the other animals for being so mean.

He made a big sign that said:

I'm Sorry!

The next day, Acting Out, the little wiggly worm went over to Raspy, the roaring lion, who by now was so hungry that his stomach was hurting.

Acting Out, the little wiggly worm asked Raspy, the roaring lion why he was so hungry. All the animals brought food to Stripe, the smelly skunk every day, just so they can drink from the Stream of love.

Acting Out asked Raspy, the roaring lion if Stripe, the smelly skunk shared his food with him. Hmmmm, that got Raspy, the roaring lion to thinking. He said that although he really only eats meat, it would have been nice if Stripe, the smelly skunk had offered or shared his food.

For the first time, Raspy, the roaring lion was thinking for himself. "You know, he said to Acting Out, the little wiggly worm, you are right. He has been eating well for three days. That is very selfish of him and I now see that he really doesn't care about me. He is only thinking about himself."

I was being mean to the other animals because I thought he really wanted to be my friend and I wanted to feel special. Now I know that good friends look out for each other. Good friends share what they have with others. Good friends treat everyone the same. They are nice all the time and to everyone.

Raspy, the roaring lion made up his mind to join the other animals in the forest of **Look and See**. He too, was going to drink with them from the Stream of Love.

Acting Out, the little wiggly worm had a meeting with all the animals, including So-so, the slithering snake and Raspy, the roaring lion.

They all decided that they would join hands and form a circle of peace and understanding around Stripe, the smelly skunk and show him what true friendship is.

All the animals were so excited that they danced around Rainbow Tree so they all could share in its beauty and joy.

Even the birds joined in with their melodies of happiness.

The next day, all the animals, including So-So, the slithering snake and Raspy, the roaring lion went to get their daily drink of water from the Stream of Love.

When Stripe, the smelly skunk saw them approaching he came out to meet them. He didn't even notice So-So, the slithering snake or Raspy, the roaring lion. He was so busy looking to see what food the animals were going to give him.

Acting Out, the little wiggly worm, greeted Stripe, the smelly skunk with the following words:

"We, the animals in the forest of **Look and See** are no longer afraid of you. You are not very nice because you do not like the way you smell. So you threaten to spray us with your gift of smell just to keep us all away."

"Grandma has told us that we all have special gifts and to be proud of who and what we are. We will no longer bring you food. We all have to find our own. That is something that we all have to do. We all drink from the Stream of Love and in doing so must learn to live to harmony."

Just then Stripe, the smelly skunk saw So-So, the slithering snake and Raspy, the roaring lion in the crowd. He became very frighten when he realized that he was all by himself. He suddenly felt the fear that he had made all the other animals in the forest of **Look and See** feel.

Acting Out, the little wiggly worm saw that Stripe, the smelly skunk was afraid. He said to Stripe, the smelly skunk, "what do you have to say for yourself? I'm sure it doesn't feel good to be afraid, does it?"

"No it doesn't said Stripe, the smelly skunk. It doesn't feel very good to be afraid. I am so sorry for my ugly behavior. I was not feeling good about myself and took it out on everyone else. What can I do to make things alright with the animals in the forest of **Look and See**?"

Well, Acting Out, the little wiggly worm said, "you have to ask the animals themselves." I do know that you should apologize for your behavior and promise not to use your special gift of smell against anyone again.

"Oh yes, said Stripe, the smelly skunk, I am so sorry and I promise never to threaten the animals in the forest of **Look and See** again."

"I will also sign a good behavior agreement. It will say that I will never bully anyone again. I will share what the forest has to offer with all the animals. I will respect myself first, which will help me to respect others for their differences and their special gifts."

GOOD BEHAVIOR AGREEMENT

- I will respect myself

- As I respect myself, I respect others for their differences and their special gifts

- I will never bully anyone again

- I will share what the forest has to offer with all the animals

- I will be a friend first.

_____

Signed by: Stripe the Skunk

Everyone was so impressed with Stripe, the smelly skunk that they all ran up to give him a hug and pat him on the back.

The animals in the forest of **Look and See** were all going to live in peace and understanding. Everyone will be able to drink equally from the Stream of Love.

Grandma, Good the Frog, and Nice, the prettiest little kitten you could ever imagine all jumped for joy.

They also rushed to Acting Out, the little wiggly worm, and congratulated him on such a wonderful plan. He solved the bullying in the forest of **Look and See** and no one got hurt.

It was a great day.

As they journey out of the forest of **Look and See,** and each headed off to their own homes, they were all so proud of themselves.

They all know that everyone has a special gift. Everyone is a little different, and the best way to have a friend is to be a friend first.

They were all so glad that their mission of stopping bullying was a wonderful success.

They couldn't wait until their next adventure. I wonder what it will be!

Questions that Grandma, Good the Frog, Acting Out, the little wiggly worm and Nice the kitten want to know.

What was the name of the book that Grandma was reading when the phone rang?

_____

_____

What lights up the Crown?

_____

_____

Who called Grandma?

_____

_____

Why?

_____

_____

What is the name of the Forest?

_____

_____

What is the name of the water that all the animals drink from?

_____

_____

Do you drink a lot of water?

_____

_____

What are the names of the animals that were being bullies?

_____

_____

Who was the ring leader?

_____

_____

What is his special gift?

_____

_____

Do you have a special gift?

_____

_____

What is it?

_____

_____

Do you have good behavior?

_____

_____

What are some of your good behaviors?

_____

_____

Are you a good friend?

_____

_____

Tell me why?

_____

_____

What are some of the things that you share with others?

_____

_____

What part of the story did you like best?

_____

_____

Why?

_____

_____

Who are some of your best friends?

_____

_____

Why?

_____

_____

What are their special gifts?

_____

_____

Acknowledgements

To my pastor Dr. Jamal-Harrison Bryant of Empowerment Temple, I thank you for making me uncomfortable until I used my gift.

To my cousin Rebecca Riddick without you these books would not have been possible.

Finally to my two best friends, Sandra Cox and Sandra Cohen, thank you for listening as I talked for I know that was not easy.

I love you all.

Phyllis L. Morris-Holmes

Printed in the United States
By Bookmasters